It all started when Jimmy go̶
Uncle Colin in America. Th̶
was unlike any bear Jimmy̶
looked tough, and he was we̶
According to the label, his name was Theodor̶
Roosevelt — T.R. for short.

Life with T.R. is quite eventful . . .

The author, Terrance Dicks, studied at
Cambridge before working as an advertising
copywriter, then a radio and television
scriptwriter and script editor. His career as a
children's author began with the Dr Who series
and he has now written many other books on
varied subjects.
ENTER T.R. is the first in a series of books
about T.R. Bear.

Also by Terrance Dicks

T.R. GOES TO SCHOOL
T.R.'s DAY OUT
T.R. AFLOAT
T.R.'s HALLOWE'EN

All published by Young Corgi Books

T.R. Bear

Enter T.R.!

T.R. Bear

Enter T.R.!

Terrance Dicks
Illustrated by
Susan Hellard

YOUNG CORGI BOOKS

T.R.BEAR
ENTER T.R.
A YOUNG CORGI BOOK   0 552 523011

PRINTING HISTORY
First published in Great Britain by Piccadilly Press
Piccadilly Press edition published 1985
Young Corgi edition published 1985
Reprinted 1987, 1988

Young Corgi Books are published by Transworld Publishers Ltd.,
61-63 Uxbridge Road, Ealing, London W5 5SA, in Australia by
Transworld Publishers (Australia) Pty. Ltd., 15-23 Helles
Avenue, Moorebank, NSW 2170, and in New Zealand by
Transworld Publishers (N.Z.) Ltd., Cnr. Moselle
and Waipareira Avenues, Henderson, Auckland.

Made and printed in Great Britain by
The Guernsey Press Co. Ltd., Guernsey, Channel Islands.

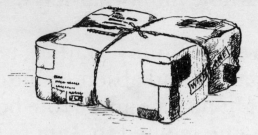

Chapter One

T. R. Arrives

It all started when Jimmy got a parcel from America. Since it was neither Christmas nor his birthday, the parcel was a surprise for everyone.

Jimmy carried the parcel up to his room to open it.

Everyone else was so curious that they all followed him, all the way up to his attic bedroom at the top of the tall old London house.

The whole family gathered round.

There was Jimmy's father, tall, bespectacled and absent-minded. He taught history and wrote books that no-one seemed to want to buy.

There was his mother, round and untidy and scatter-brained.

She made pots and vases and dishes in a kiln at the bottom of the garden.

The pottery was so strangely shaped, that no-one seemed to want to buy them either.

There was Jimmy's elder brother George, wearing glasses like his father, and trying to look serious and important and grown-up.

And finally his sister Jenny, younger than George but older than Jimmy, who secretly thought she was the nicest and most sensible and most really grown-up of the entire family.

Even Harbottle, the dog was there.

He was called Harbottle because he was large and hairy and shapeless, exactly like Professor Harbottle at the college where Jimmy's father taught history,

part-time.

'Well, come on then,' said George impatiently. 'We haven't got all day.'

George was always saying things like that.

'Nobody asked you up here anyway,' thought Jimmy.

As usual, Jimmy didn't say any of this out loud. Instead, he just got on with opening his parcel.

It wasn't easy.

There was lots of string and sellotape.

Lots of thick brown paper around a cardboard box.

Tissue paper *inside* the box.

At last inside the box there was a bear.

It was a teddy bear. But somehow it wasn't quite like any other bear he'd ever seen.

It was smallish and broad shouldered.

Instead of the gentle, amiable air of most teddy bears, this bear had a kind of determined almost scowling expression. This bear looked tough — despite the fact that it was wearing glasses, small, perfectly round ones with black wire frames.

'Surely a bear can't need glasses,' thought Jimmy.

Then he realised that the spectacles had no glass in them.

There was a letter on top of the bear.

Jimmy took it out of the box and handed it to his mother. 'Read it out, Mum.'

His mother looked at the letter. 'It's from your Uncle Colin in Connecticut.'

Jimmy's mother's brother was a history professor who had taken a job in an American University.

She began to read.

'Dear Jimmy,
We found this teddy bear in the attic of the house we just bought over here. As we bought the house and all its contents, I guess he's ours. As you know, our kids are all grown up so we thought you might like to have him.

All the best to you and the family.

Love,

Uncle Colin.'

Jimmy's mother peered at the letter through her glasses – round ones rather like the bear's except hers were gold rimmed.

'Oh, there's a P. S. According to the label on the box, his name is Theodore Roosevelt Bear. Bit of a mouthful, that. You could call him

T.R. for short.'

Jimmy looked down at the bear.

Lying in his box of tissue paper, the bear looked rather as if it was asleep in bed.

Just to try out the sound of it, Jimmy said, 'T.R. Bear!'

The bear woke up. Its eyes opened wide behind the round spectacle-frames. It yawned and stretched, and sat up, looking the astonished Jimmy straight in the eye.

'Hi there, kid,' said T.R. Bear. 'How ya doing?'

Chapter Two

T.R. Meets The Toys

Everyone stared at the teddy bear in amazement.

Jimmy was just as surprised as everyone else — but he wasn't too surprised to notice something else.

He saw that the teddy bear was just as surprised as the people around it. It looked round with an air of utter astonishment, made a noise that sounded something like 'Urrk!' and collapsed backwards into the box.

9

There was a moment of silence.

Jimmy's father said, 'Amazing! What will they think of next.'

'But it *talked*,' said his mother. 'And it sat up!'

'Voice activated tape recorder probably', said George airily. He always liked to have the explanation for everything.

Jenny said, 'Try it again, Jimmy.'

'Hello, T.R. Bear!' said Jimmy.

The teddy bear didn't move or speak. It lay in its box, clearly a toy bear and nothing more.

George said, 'I imagine the battery must have run down. After all, if it's been stuck away in an attic for ages . . .'

They all prodded and poked the bear for a bit, but they couldn't feel anything that felt like machinery inside.

George wanted to take it apart and try and mend it, but Jimmy wouldn't let him.

After a bit everyone lost interest and drifted off.

As she went out Jenny whispered, 'Never mind, Jimmy. I daresay he'll talk again when he feels like it.'

Left alone, Jimmy examined the bear a bit longer. Once or twice he tried shouting 'Hello T.R!' very loudly, but it didn't do any good. Finally he put T.R. on the shelf, between two of his other toys. One was a teddy bear called Edward that he'd had since he was very small.

The other was a rag doll called Sally Ann. She was Jenny's doll really. Although Jenny felt she'd

outgrown her, she was too fond of
the doll either to throw or give it
away.

So Sally Ann had been moved
into Jimmy's room. Jenny said she
would be company for Edward.

For ages now they had sat on the
toy shelf side by side. The long wide
shelf ran along the end of Jimmy's
room, just above the bookcase, next
to the cage with the gerbils. By

raising his head a little Jimmy could
see the rag doll and the teddy bear
sitting side by side, just before he
went to sleep.

T.R. was still on the shelf with the
others, when it was time for Jimmy
to go to bed.

That night Jimmy discovered
that the rest of his toys could talk as
well.

He must have fallen asleep and
woken up again.

He was laying in bed in a sort of
drifting doze when he heard a
drawling voice say, 'But my dear
fellow, really! How could you?'

Somehow he knew at once that it
was Edward Bear speaking.
Edward was a very aristocratic
looking teddy bear, tall and thin. As
a matter of fact, the voice sounded

very like Prince Charles.

A second voice said reproachfully. 'You spoke — in front of humans. It's breaking all the rules.'

This was a female voice, very clipped and efficient, and Jimmy knew at once it just had to be Sally Ann.

Jimmy lifted his head a little and half-opened his eyes. Then he lay quite still in bed, listening hard.

He heard the deep, rumbling voice of T.R. 'Listen, give me a break! You guys never heard of jet lag? For years I get stuck in an attic, then I get thrown in a box and whizzed over the Atlantic. So naturally, when I wake up I'm a little confused. Could happen to anybody.'

'Nonsense,' said Sally Ann
severely. 'The rules are perfectly
clear. No moving or talking unless
the humans are asleep, and we're
all alone.'

'One simply must have proper
standards of behaviour, old chap,'
said Edward severely.

15

T.R. sounded as if he was getting impatient. 'Okay, okay,' he rumbled. 'I apologise. It should never have happened, but it did, and I can't make it un-happen.'

'Now the humans know you can talk,' said Sally Ann worriedly. 'They might even begin to guess about the rest of us.'

T.R. wasn't worried. 'Listen, lady, let me tell you something about humans. They believe what they *wanna* believe. Likewise, they don't believe what they *don't* wanna believe. And no human wants to believe in talking toys. You saw what happened. They've already convinced themselves that I'm some kind of mechanical gizmo. Pretty soon they'll forget the whole thing. Trust me.'

16

'Well, I just hope you're right, old fellow,' said Edward. 'We'll just have to overlook it — after all, you are an *American* bear. I suppose we should expect some strange behaviour.

'Oh yeah? And what's so strange about an American bear?'

'Teddy bears are British,' said Edward positively. 'Everyone knows that.'

'Horse feathers,' snorted T.R.

'I'm afraid I must agree with Edward,' said Sally Ann. 'The teddy bear is a traditionally British institution.'

'That's just where you're wrong,' said T.R. triumphantly. 'Teddy bears are as American as apple pie. Where do you think the name comes from? Theodore Roosevelt, that's who! And I guess you know who he was?'

Edward looked blank.

Sally Ann said, 'Of course I know. We dolls aren't stupid, you know. He was one of your Presidents, wasn't he?'

'That's right. Greatest President the US of A ever had!'

'How did *we* get his name?' asked Edward now overcome with curiosity.

T.R. leaned back. 'Story goes that Teddy Roosevelt was out hunting one day when he came across a bear cub that had lost its mother. Teddy said it was too small to shoot, and let it go. Some guy drew a picture in the papers and called it Teddy's bear. Then some other guy with a little toyshop made a bear and put it

in the window.' T.R. paused
impressively. 'The rest is history.'
He waved a paw at Edward. 'So you
see, buster, you're not just a teddy
bear, you're a Teddy Roosevelt
Bear—just like me!'

'Good Lord,' said Edward softly.
'Well, who'd have thought it. We're
practically related. Welcome to
Britain, old chap! Allow me to
present my friend Sally Ann.'

T.R. got up on his stubby little legs and bowed politely. 'My pleasure, ma'am.'

Sally Ann stretched out her thin rag arm, and T.R. bent over and kissed her hand.

'Charmed I'm sure,' said Sally Ann, slightly taken aback.

'Now then,' said Edward politely. 'Do tell us about your trip.'

Before T.R. could reply a great black shape sprang through the window and landed in the centre of the room with a soft thud.

Moonlight glinted on huge green eyes. Jimmy realised with horror that it was the big black wild cat that lived in the grounds of the nearby church.

He knew what it wanted, too.

It was after his gerbils.

It had got in the room jumping
from the overhanging tree branch
and attacked them once before. It
had knocked the cage from the
shelf so that the door sprang open.

Only the fact that George in the
next room had heard the crash and
come running in, had saved the
gerbils from being the black cat's

supper. The black cat had escaped through the window that time. Now it had come back to try again.

The gerbils knew it too.

A frantic alarm — drumming came from their cage.

The great black shape stalked across the floor towards them.

It crouched, ready to spring, tail lashing gently to and fro.

Chapter Three

T.R. To The Rescue

Jimmy wanted to get up and chase the cat away, but he seemed frozen with fear.

The wild cat was a big strong animal, and it was very dangerous. It had a habit of coming into people's houses and stealing food from their pet cats, attacking any cat who dared to stop it. Even quite big dogs had come off worse in fights, and a man from the Council who had tried to catch it had been badly scratched.

Before Jimmy could move, T.R. Bear was in action.

He sprang from the shelf, landing on top of the wild cat, knocking it flying.

The cat leaped back hissing, and T.R. rolled over and jumped back onto his feet.

He marched steadily towards the cat, paws raised like a boxer.

The cat lashed out at him, and T.R. dodged and jabbed it hard on the end of the nose.

Again, the cat hissed and retreated.

But not very far.

It crouched, sizing up its strange

opponent, and then began stalking forwards again.

Claws out, it aimed a slashing blow at T.R. who jumped back just in time.

There was a second thump as Edward Bear jumped from the toy shelf, landing on the other side of the cat.

The cat swung round — and T.R.

darted forwards and cuffed it across the ear.

The wild cat hissed angrily. It swung its head to and fro, confused, wondering which of its two enemies to attack.

Jimmy knew that whichever bear it chose was in grave danger of being ripped to shreds by those terrible claws.

Suddenly there was the most tremendous clanging and clattering.

Sally Ann had pushed an old biscuit tin full of plastic toys off the shelf.

Frightened by the sudden noise, the wild cat gave a screech of alarm and disappeared out of the window.

T.R. looked at Sally Ann who was

peering over the edge of the shelf. 'Well done, lady. That fixed him. Bully for you!'

'Hear! Hear!' said Edward. 'Jolly quick thinking. And you should be congratulated, too, old chap. Bravest thing I ever saw.'

T.R. sounded almost embarrassed. 'Heck, it was nothing. A bear's gotta do what a bear's gotta do. I was mighty glad when you arrived to back me up.'

'Oh, I didn't do anything really,' said Edward modestly. 'You were the one who jumped straight in. Well done, old chap, I'm proud to shake your paw.'

Solemnly, the two bears touched paws.

There was a pounding of feet on the stairs.

The door was opened and the
light switched on and suddenly the
room was full of people, Mother
and Father and George and Jenny
all in pyjamas and nightdresses.
Last of all came Harbottle, barking
excitedly.

'What on earth's going on?'
asked mother.

Jimmy sat up in bed. 'It was that black wild cat, after my gerbils again,' he said sleepily. 'But don't worry, T.R. chased it off. Edward and Sally Ann helped too.'

Everyone looked around the room. T.R. and Edward Bear lay sprawled out on the floor, surrounded by plastic toys, while Sally Ann lay in a heap on the shelf.

'I see what happened,' said George importantly, coming up with the wrong answer as usual. 'The cat must have jumped in the window, and knocked over the toys and that tin. The noise frightened it, and it cleared off.'

Everyone agreed that this was the only possible explanation.

Everyone joined in putting the plastic toys back in the tin, and

Edward Bear and T.R. and Sally
Ann were rearranged on their
shelf.

The window was closed a bit
more, leaving just a tiny gap at the
top and everyone trooped off,
telling Jimmy there was no need to
worry.

His mother and father and Jenny
kissed him goodnight, George
patted him on the shoulder, and
Harbottle licked his ear. Strangely
enough, Jimmy wasn't worried at
all.

Not with T.R. to look after him.

And it was nice that T.R. had
made friends with the other toys he
thought.

He really must persuade T.R. to
talk again.

Jimmy felt sure that T.R. was the

sort of bear you could rely on for good advice.

Perhaps if he got him off alone somewhere . . .

Still thinking and planning, Jimmy drifted off to sleep.

Chapter Four
T.R.'s Plan

Next morning, Sunday, Jimmy woke as usual, long before anyone else. He got up, put on his dressing gown, and went downstairs to make himself some breakfast.

He took T.R. Bear with him.

Everyone was asleep, and the house was quiet and still.

Jimmy went down to the kitchen and sat T.R. down on the table. He stood on a chair and got cornflakes from the top cupboard, collected a bowl and a spoon and milk from the fridge.

Jimmy sat down, and sat T.R. Bear on the table in front of him.

The stocky little bear's eyes gazed blankly at him from behind the empty wire spectacle frames.

'Now come off it, T.R.' said Jimmy firmly. 'You know you can talk, I know you can talk, and you know I know you can talk.' Jimmy paused for a moment wondering if that had come out quite right. Then he went on. 'You talked when you first arrived here, and I heard you and the other toys last night, when you saved my gerbils from that cat

—thanks very much, by the way.
Now then, why don't you talk now?
There's no-one about.'

For a moment nothing
happened.

T.R. stared glassily back at him,
quite clearly nothing more than an
ordinary toy bear.

Jimmy even began to wonder if
he'd imagined the whole thing.

Maybe there *was* some kind of run down tape recorder and clockwork inside the bear.

Perhaps he'd dreamed everything that happened last night.

Perhaps the cat *had* jumped through the window and knocked over the tin, just as George had said.

Then, suddenly, wonderfully, a twinkle came into T.R.'s eyes, and his deep gravelly voice rumbled, 'Okay kid, you win. What the heck! You couldn't spare a glass of milk and a cookie, could you?'

A few minutes later Jimmy and T.R. were having breakfast together.

'I didn't expect you to eat as well as talk,' said Jimmy.

T.R. peered at him over his glasses. 'When I'm awake I eat — when I'm asleep I don't — just like you!'

'Do all toys come to life when their owners aren't around?'

T.R. shook his head. 'Nope. Some do, some don't. Depends.'

'Depends on what?'

'On the humans. See, we toys take our life from you humans. We kind of live off the extra energy. You're our batteries. Now, a family with a lot of life and love in it, like yours, there's plenty of life to go round for the toys as well. Some places there's barely enough for the humans, let alone the toys. Depends.'

'So a toy that isn't loved and looked after will probably never

come to life — and one that
somebody loves is almost sure to?'

'You got it, kid!' How about
another cookie?'

'Sure thing,' said Jimmy. He got
down and went over to the biscuit
tin.

But when he got back to the
table, T.R. was sitting up stiffly
again, staring glassily ahead.

'T.R.! What is it?' said Jimmy in
alarm.

There were footsteps on the
stairs and his mother and father
came into the kitchen, both in
pyjamas and dressing gowns.

They looked in surprise at
Jimmy, and at the biscuits and milk
in front of T.R.

Then his mother smiled. 'I see
your new friend is having breakfast

with you, Jimmy.' She turned to his father and whispered, 'Look, he's even drunk some of the milk and half-eaten the biscuit. Isn't that sweet?'

Jimmy held his breath, hoping she wouldn't notice that a few biscuit crumbs and a drop or two of milk were still clinging to the fur around T.R.'s mouth.

But his mother turned away and began making toast and coffee.

Jimmy gave a sigh of relief, realising that what T.R. had said last night was quite true.

People would always find explanations for things they just didn't want to believe.

Jimmy's father went to the front door to get the papers and brought them back to the table.

But instead of disappearing inside them as he usually did he just sat staring glumly at the still-folded papers.

'What's the matter, Dad?' asked Jimmy.

'Oh nothing . . .'

Jimmy's mother believed you should answer children properly and not fob them off. She said how

could they grow up sensible if
no-one told them anything?'

So *she* answered Jimmy's
question. 'Your father's worried
because his publisher still won't
make up his mind about his latest
book.'

'The new history text book you
mean?'

Jimmy's father nodded gloomily.
'That's the one!'

Jimmy's father believed that a lot of children's history books made history boring when it should have been exciting. So he had written one of his own, showing history as real people with real problems, just like life today.

The book had been rejected by several publishers, but finally someone had said it was an interesting idea, and they might publish it — but then again they might not.

The trouble was that the someone — apparently his name was Mr Witherspoon — just wouldn't make up his mind.

'You really ought to phone him again,' said Jimmy's mother.

'Well, I've tried but whenever I call him at the office, his secretary says he's in a meeting.'

'Do you know where he lives?'

Jimmy's father fished inside the bulging folder by the phone where business papers were kept.

'It's on his letter, I think. Yes, look there's a business and a home number.'

'Why not ring him now, then?'

Jimmy's father was shocked. 'Oh, I couldn't bother him on a Sunday. It wouldn't be fair. Maybe there'll be a letter or a phone call in the morning.'

Hurriedly he picked up the paper and began to read.

Jimmy and his mother exchanged looks.

Jimmy's father was as nice a man as you could ever meet, but sometimes he was too nice for his own good. He hated to upset anybody, or give anyone trouble.

It was typical of him that although this man Witherspoon had been keeping him waiting for weeks, he wouldn't think of bothering him on a Sunday morning.

Jimmy's father put down the paper. 'It really would be wonderful if they did publish my book. It would help at the college too.' Jimmy's father explained that there was a promotion coming up, and old Harbottle, the Professor not the dog, would be impressed. He picked up the paper again.

Jimmy finished his breakfast and went upstairs to get dressed.

As he picked up T.R. a voice from nowhere whispered in his ear,

'Grab that letter, kid!'

Jimmy picked up the letter, pretended to put it back in the file and stuck it inside his pyjama jacket and hurried from the room.

Chapter Five

T.R. Steps In

When they were back in his bedroom Jimmy said, 'What did you want the letter for?'

T.R. came to life again. 'Because we're gonna put a rocket under this guy Witherspoon!'

'How?'

'Is there another phone?'

'There's one in the sitting room.'

'Lead me to it.'

Jimmy carried T.R. into the sitting room. It was empty, since everyone was either still in bed or pottering round in the kitchen.

'Right,' said T.R. 'You dial the number, then hold the phone so I can talk.'

Jimmy dialled. As soon as the phone rang at the other end, he handed the phone to T.R. keeping his own ear close to the receiver.

The phone rang and rang. At last a sleepy voice answered, 'Yes? Wassermatter?'

Jimmy realised it was still quite early on Sunday morning. They must have woken Mr Witherspoon up.

T.R. produced a strange series of beeps and clicks and then spoke in a high-pitched voice. 'Is that Mr

Witherspoon? This is the New York operator here. We have a call for you.'

T.R. produced a few more clicks and then spoke in his own deep, rumbling voice. 'Witherspoon? T.R. Bear here. Bear of Anglo Amalgamated Consolidated Publishing U.S.A. and U.K. You've heard of me?'

'Yes, of course, Mr. Bear,' said Witherspoon.

Of course he hadn't, but T.R. sounded so important that Witherspoon thought he'd better play safe.

'It's about this book, Witherspoon,' growled T.R.

'What book, sir?'

T.R. glanced worriedly at Jimmy, who held up the letter and pointed. 'A New Approach to History,' said T.R. 'Now listen Witherspoon. Anglo Amalgamated Consolidated want that book. Best thing to come along in years. Now, are you buying it, or aren't you? Because if you're not, then I'm catching the first plane to London to sign up the writer for a whole series!'

There was an astonished pause

then a triumphant voice said, 'I'm afraid you're too late, Mr. Bear. My firm has just decided to publish. I spoke to the writer a little while ago.'

('Big liar,' thought Jimmy.)

'You're sure?' said T.R. disappointedly.

'Quite sure, Mr. Bear,' said Witherspoon smugly. 'I'm afraid you've missed the bus on this one. We're not so slow as all that in Old England. We know a good thing when we see it.'

'Okay Witherspoon, you win,' said T.R. in a disgusted voice. 'Nice talking to you, have a nice day.'

He nodded to Jimmy, who slammed down the phone.

'What was all that about?' asked Jimmy.

T.R. chuckled. 'Way I see it, this guy's a ditherer. One sure way to convince him the book's good is to make it look like someone else wants it.'

Suddenly the door opened.

It was Jimmy's mother. 'Who were you phoning, dear?'

'Oh, just one of my friends,' said Jimmy, keeping his fingers crossed behind his back.

'I thought I heard another voice — an American one.'

'Oh, that was just me! We were messing about doing funny voices.' Jimmy crossed his fingers harder than ever.

Suddenly the telephone rang.

Jimmy's mother picked it up and listened. 'Yes? Yes, he's here.' She went to the door and called,

'Telephone for you, darling.'

Jimmy's father hurried up the stairs.

He took the phone and stood listening, his expression growing more and more astonished. 'Yes? Yes, *really*? That's very good news. No, I haven't accepted any other offers. Yes, I'll see you on Monday. Goodbye!'

He put down the phone and turned to Jimmy's mother with an expression of utter amazement. 'That was Witherspoon. He likes the history book and he's decided to publish. He wants me to go to his office on Monday and sign the contract.

He's taking me out to lunch!'

There was a great deal of excitement after that, as everyone

in the family was told the good
news.

Jimmy's father was so pleased
and excited that he decided to take
the whole family out to lunch, at the
local pizza restaurant.

To everyone's surprise
Jimmy insisted on taking T.R. Bear
to the celebration. He sat him up at
the table with a glass of coke and a
slice of pizza in front of him.

Everyone was so busy talking and
laughing and congratulating
Jimmy's father on his success that
no-one paid much attention to the
little teddy bear.

The next time Jimmy glanced
across at T.R., the coke glass was
half empty and the pizza had
disappeared.

Jimmy looked at T.R. and, just

for a moment, he could have sworn
he saw him wink.

Jimmy sat back, munching his
pizza contentedly.

Life with T.R. Bear, he decided,
was going to be a lot of fun.

T.R. GOES TO SCHOOL
by Terrance Dicks

'You won't hear a peep out of me, kid,' promises T.R. Bear when Jimmy decides to take him to school for show and tell. The trouble is that T.R. is a rather excitable bear and tends to break the rules . . .

T.R.'s visit to school turns out to be a day that Jimmy would never forget

0 552 52302X

YOUNG CORGI

T.R.'s DAY OUT
by Terrance Dicks

When Jimmy's school arranges a day
trip to a museum, T.R. and the other
toys insist Jimmy takes them along with
him. There are lots of things they want
to see, too! With T.R. along, Jimmy's
trip becomes the most exciting day out
ever . . .

0 552 523569

YOUNG
CORGI

T.R. BEAR:
T.R. AFLOAT
by Terrance Dicks

'Sixteen men on a dead man's chest,' sang T.R. Bear. 'Yo ho ho and a bottle of rum!'

Jimmy and T.R. are on holiday at last. On a boat! The drive down and the first night on board are quite an adventure in themselves. But there's more excitement in store when T.R. overhears two men plotting to steal some rare birds' eggs from the island nature reserve.

He's determined to catch them red-handed. All he needs is a plan . . .

0 552 524654

YOUNG
CORGI

If you would like to receive a newsletter telling you about our new children's books, fill in the coupon with your name and address and send it to:

The Childrens Books Editor
Transworld Publishers Ltd.,
61/63 Uxbridge Road, Ealing,
London, W5 5SA

Name ....

Address ....

....

....